Dear Parent:
Your child's love of reading starts here!

Every child learns to read in a different way and at his or her own speed. You can help your young reader improve and become more confident by encouraging his or her own interests and abilities. You can also guide your child's spiritual development by reading stories with biblical values and Bible stories, like I Can Read! books published by Zonderkidz. From books your child reads with you to the first books he or she reads alone, there are I Can Read! books for every stage of reading:

SHARED READING
Basic language, word repetition, and whimsical illustrations, ideal for sharing with your emergent reader.

BEGINNING READING
Short sentences, familiar words, and simple concepts for children eager to read on their own.

READING WITH HELP
Engaging stories, longer sentences, and language play for developing readers.

READING ALONE
Complex plots, challenging vocabulary, and high-interest topics for the independent reader.

ADVANCED READING
Short paragraphs, chapters, and exciting themes for the perfect bridge to chapter books.

I Can Read! books have introduced children to the joy of reading since 1957. Featuring award-winning authors and illustrators and a fabulous cast of beloved characters, I Can Read! books set the standard for beginning readers.

A lifetime of discovery begins with the magical words **"I Can Read!"**

Visit www.icanread.com for information on enriching your child's reading experience.
Visit www.zonderkidz.com for more Zonderkidz I Can Read! titles.

Even though I walk
through the darkest valley,
I will fear no evil,
for you are with me.
—Psalm 23:4

ZONDERKIDZ

Copyright © 2015 by Berenstain Publishing, Inc.
Illustrations © 2015 by Berenstain Publishing, Inc.

Requests for information should be addressed to:
Zonderkidz, 3900 Sparks Dr. SE, Grand Rapids, Michigan 49546

ISBN: 978-0-310-62376-2 (hardcover)

Faith Gets Us Through ISBN 9780310725015 Copyright © 2012 by Berenstain Publishing, Inc.
Thank God for Good Health ISBN 9780310725039 Copyright © 2013 by Berenstain Publishing, Inc.
Piggy Bank Blessings ISBN 9780310725053 Copyright © 2013 by Berenstain Publishing, Inc.
God Made the Colors ISBN 9780310725077 Copyright © 2013 by Berenstain Publishing, Inc.
God Made the Seasons ISBN 9780310725091 Copyright © 2012 by Berenstain Publishing, Inc.
Do Not Fear, God Is Near ISBN 9780310725114 Copyright © 2013 by Berenstain Publishing, Inc.

Editor: Mary Hassinger
Design: Diane Mielke

Printed in Mexico

15 16 17 18 19 • 11 10 9 8 7 6 5 4 3 2 1

ZONDERkidz

I Can Read!

BEGINNING
1
READING

The Berenstain Bears
Faith Gets Us Through

Story and Pictures By
Stan & Jan Berenstain with Mike Berenstain

Today was a special day.

The Bear Scouts were going to

Spooky Cave.

They wanted to earn their

Cave Adventure Merit Badges.

Scout Sister said, "I am a little scared."

Scout Brother said, "Me, too."

Scout Fred said, "As the Bible says,

'The Lord is my light and my salvation

—whom shall I fear?'"

Spooky Cave looked spooky!

It looked like a big, open mouth

with big, sharp teeth.

Scout Papa said, "Come on, scouts.

Don't be scared.

All we need is a little faith.

Let's earn those badges."

Mountain goats watched Papa
and the scouts go into the cave.

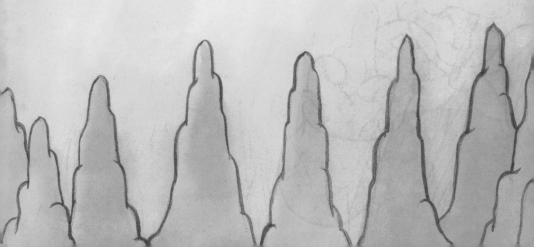

Scouts Papa, Brother, Sister, and Fred
went in Spooky Cave.

Papa said, "If you have a question,
just ask me.

I know all about caves."

Sister asked,

"What are these pointy things?"

Fred said,
"Some of those pointy
things grow up and
some grow down."

Papa said, "Yes. Listen to this rhyme—
Stalactites and stalagmites,
Only caves got 'em.
Tites are up on top.
Mites are on the bottom."

The scouts looked up.

They looked down.

God made amazing things!

Then Sister said,

"It sounds funny in the cave."

Papa said, "I know all about caves,

so let me tell you.

It sounds funny because there is an

echo in the cave.

Listen."

Papa shouted, "HELLO!"

The scouts heard the sound bounce

off the cave walls.

'HELLO! Hello! Hello!'

went the echo.

But Papa forgot that noises in a cave can shake things loose.

"Be strong and courageous," Fred quoted from the Bible. "And look out!"

"YIPE!" said Papa.

A falling stalactite just missed him!

Papa and the scouts went
deeper into the cave.
The scouts said a prayer to
keep up their courage.

Soon, they could not
remember which
way they had
come.

Sister asked, "Are we lost?"

Papa said, "We are not lost.

I know all about caves so

I left a trail of string."

But Papa did not know a goat

had followed them.

The goat had eaten the trail of string.

The scouts asked, "What will we do?"

Papa said, "Never fear!

I know all about caves."

Papa got his finger wet. He held it up.

"I feel a breeze," said Papa.

"That means there is another way out."

But Papa did not know about

the stream in Spooky Cave.

"Yiiieee!" shouted Papa, as he fell in the water.

"Lord, help us!" prayed the scouts.

Down,

down

they went.

Down,

down,

down ...

... and out of

Spooky Cave.

God kept them safe.
The scouts were
back outside!

Papa said, "Here are your Cave

Adventure Merit Badges."

Fred said, "Our faith and prayers
sure helped us get through."

Sister said, "It was fun."

Brother said, "Just like a water slide."

"Scout Papa, may we go back
in the cave?" Fred asked.

Papa said, "Scouts, I know all about caves.
I am glad you asked that question.
The answer is …

But the scouts were happy.

They were happy they had faith.

They were happy they had their badges.

They were happy Papa knew
everything about caves.

Well ...

almost everything.

Do not be wise in your own eyes;
fear the Lord and shun evil.
This will bring health to your body
and nourishment to your bones.

—Proverbs 3:7-8

The Berenstain Bears

Thank God for Good Health

Story and Pictures By

Stan & Jan Berenstain with Mike Berenstain

"The doctor?" said Brother and Sister.
"Why?"

"It is time for a check-up,"
said Mama.

"A check-up?"

said Brother.

"Phooey!"

"A check-up helps make sure

you stay well," said Mama.

Then she put on her hat.

"Papa and I pray to God for good health every day," said Mama. "Now, come along."

"Mama? Papa? Will Dr. Grizzly

give us a shot?" Brother asked.

Mama said, "Maybe a booster shot."

"Stop!" said Sister when they were

on their way. "This is the wrong road."

Papa said, "This is the right road."

"Turn back!" said Brother.

"I saw a lost dog."

Papa said, "There was no lost dog."

The Bears got to

Dr. Grizzly's office.

"What a crowd," said Brother.

"We will be here all day."

"Patience is a virtue," said Mama. "The Good Book says, 'A person's wisdom yields patience.'"

It was Brother and Sister's turn.

"Hello," said Dr. Gert Grizzly.

"It's time for your

check-ups."

"Hop up, Sister.
It is your turn first,"
said Dr. Grizzly.

"Let me check your tummy," she said.

"Please tell me if it hurts."

"Well," said Dr. Grizzly.

"What do you say?"

"No problem," said Sister.

"Very good," said the doctor.

"What is that?" asked Brother.

Brother was pointing at

something the doctor was holding.

"It is one of my tools.

It is a stethoscope.

It lets me listen to

your heart,"

said the doctor.

"Now for your ears," said Dr. Grizzly.

"I hope they are clean,"
said Sister.

"Just fine!
Now tell me what you hear
when I whisper,"
said the doctor.

"You said, 'So far, so good,'
said the cubs.

"Hear that, Mama?" asked Papa.
"God has blessed our cubs
with good health."

"Now your eyes," said Dr. Grizzly.

"Please read the small letters."

"A, P, R, I, O, U, Z," said both cubs.

"Very good! The Bible says,

'If your eyes are healthy,

your whole body will be full of light.'"

"Next, step on the scale," said the doctor.

"We will check your weight."

"Thirty-seven for Sister and forty-six for Brother.

"I am proud of you both," said Dr. Grizzly. "You have taken good care of your bodies. God has blessed you with good health."

Papa said, "Those cubs
are just like old Papa Q. Bear—
very healthy!

Now … may I get weighed?"
"Of course," said Dr. Grizzly.

The doctor looked at the scale.

"Well, Papa," said the doctor,

"God is looking after the cubs but

you need to start looking after you!"

"Thank you, Dr. Grizzly,"
said Brother and Sister.
"So long!"

"Wait just a minute. I almost forgot.
You both need a booster shot,"
said the doctor.

"But," said Sister,
"if we are healthy, why do
we need a shot?"

"This special shot keeps you healthy,"
Dr. Grizzly said.

Sister was first.

"This may hurt for half a minute," said the doctor.

But it was not bad!

"Are you brave like Sister?"

Dr. Grizzly asked Brother.

And he was.

"One more thing," said
the doctor. She found her
prescription pad
and wrote.

"Is that for bad-tasting
medicine?" asked Sister.
"No, this is for Papa."

"Carrot sticks, anyone?"

Papa asked at dessert that day.

"No thanks," said Brother.

"Well, Lord," said Papa.

"We give thanks for all your blessings—
including carrot sticks!"

Whoever gathers money little by little makes it grow.
—*Proverbs 13:11*

The Berenstain Bears®

PIGGY BANK BLESSINGS

Story and Pictures By

Stan & Jan Berenstain with Mike Berenstain

Brother and Sister Bear liked shopping
with Mama.

One day, Brother saw a toy he wanted.

Brother said, "May I have that toy plane?"

Mama said, "Yes."

Sister saw a teddy bear.

Sister said, "May I have that teddy?"

Mama said, "Yes."

But Mama did not say yes all the time.

"I want that truck too,"

Brother said.

Mama said, "No, not today."

"Why not?" asked Brother.

"You cannot have all the things

you want," said Mama.

"Why?" asked Sister.

Then Mama had an idea.

Mama bought a bank.

She said, "I will teach you

about money."

The new bank looked like a small pig.

It had a slot for money.

"The Bible says we should all

set aside some money.

This will help you save,"

Mama said.

Mama told the cubs about
saving money for something special.
She told them when they got money
as gifts it should go in the bank.

Sometimes
they got pennies.

Sometimes
they got nickels …

or dimes …

or quarters.

And sometimes
they got dollar bills!

Brother and Sister got money

for the jobs they did.

They emptied trash.

They watered flowers.

They pulled weeds.

Mama had told them
they should save for
something special.
And that is just what
the cubs did.

One day Mama said, "You cubs are doing a good job saving."

"Thank you," said Sister.

"But when we want to use it for something special, how will we get the money out?"

Mama said, "You will know when the time comes."

Then one day, Brother and Sister
knew the time had come.
They needed the money for
something special.
Sister said, "Now how do we
get the money out?"

"There's only one way
to do it," Brother said.

He got his toy hammer.

CRASH went the piggy bank.

The money spilled out.

Brother and Sister took their money.

They ran out of the tree house.

Later, Mama saw the broken bank.

"Oh dear," said Mama.

"As Proverbs says, 'Cast but a glance at riches

and they are gone, for they will surely

sprout wings and fly off …'" she said.

"I hope they are using their

money wisely.

Just then, the door opened.

In came Brother and Sister.

They each had a huge lollipop.

"Cubs!" Mama said.

"You were saving for something special."

Mama did not see the small

box the cubs were hiding.

"We did, Mama," Sister said.

Mama said, "Lollipops are not special!"
She did not think Brother and Sister
had learned all about saving.

"We know," said Brother.
"But YOU are special, Mama,"
said Sister.
"Here is your birthday gift."

Mama said, "Oh dear!

It IS my birthday tomorrow.

May I open it now?"

"Yes!" said the cubs.

Mama's gift was a watch.

She was thankful to God

for her two loving cubs.

"What a fine gift," said Mama.

"Thank you.

But where did you get the lollipops?"

Brother said, "We got your watch
at Mr. Jones' store.
He gave them to us for being
such nice cubs."

"Mr. Jones is right about that.
You are nice cubs," said Mama.
"And like the Good Book says,
'their children will be a blessing.'"

And Mama gave Brother and Sister
a big bear hug.

"I have set my rainbow in the clouds."
— Genesis 9:13

ZONDERkidz I Can Read!™
BEGINNING 1 READING

The Berenstain Bears®
God Made the Colors

Story and Pictures By
Stan & Jan Berenstain with Mike Berenstain

We love colors—colors God made.

God made every single shade.

Red, red, we love red

like that barn painted bright barn red,

and that woodpecker's

bright red head.

Yellow, yellow!

We love yellow!

The color of the sun,

its brightest beam.

The yummy color

of lemon ice cream.

Do we love blue?

You bet we do!

The color of God's sky? Yes.

The color of Mama's

polka-dot dress.

But God made other colors too.

They come from mixing

yellow, red, and blue.

Mix red and yellow,

and what do you get?

Orange! Orange

is what you get.

God mixed colors and made them glow.

He made bright orange for nature's show.

The color of a leaf about to drop,

the color of a farmer's pumpkin crop.

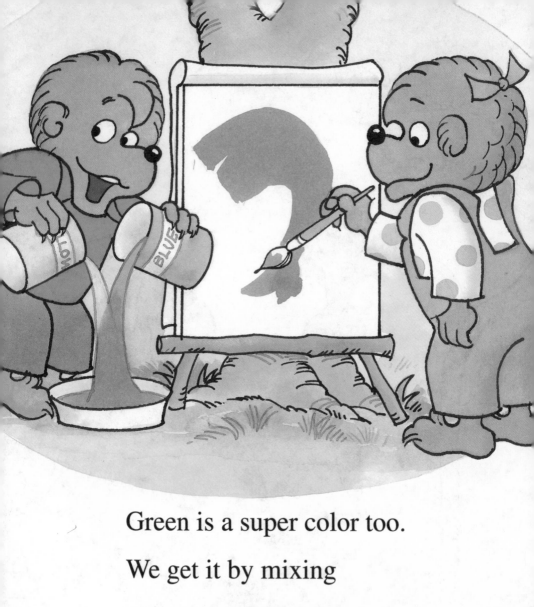

Green is a super color too.

We get it by mixing

yellow and blue.

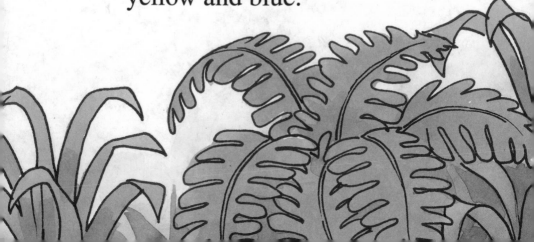

We love green. How about you?

It seems to be God's favorite too.

It's the color of nature all around,

of most things that grow

out of the ground.

Though all greens share
a single name,
all greens are not
the very same.

Some are dark.

Some are light.

Some are dull and

some are bright.

The fact, friends,
is also true
of all the other
colors too.

Colors, colors!

Dull and bright.

God made colors,

dark and light.

Wait! What about purple
which don't forget,
is also known as violet?

We get purple,
rich and fine,
when red and blue
we combine.

It is the color of grapes

on the vine.

The color of feet

that make grape wine.

We love yellow,

red, and blue.

We love green

and orange too.

And purple, of course,

which don't forget,

is also known as violet.

PAINT AND HA

BEIGE TAN

BUFF BROWN

We see those colors
and lots more
at the paint
and hardware store.

Beige and tan,
buff and brown,
the colors of the bears
in our town.

God made bears and people too
of different color, different hue.

We love the color of every bear.

And the color of people

everywhere.

God paints sunsets at the end of day.

At night the colors

all fade away.

It grows dark,

and darker still.

Will the colors come back?

Yes! Yes!

Yes, they will.

God makes the dawn of

another day.

The sun comes up.

Hooray! Hooray!

We get up, go out, and say …

God made the colors
red, yellow, and blue.
We love green
and orange too.
And purple, of course,
which don't forget,
is also called violet.

There is a time for everything,
and a season for every
activity under the heavens.

—*Ecclesiastes 3:1*

ZONDERkidz **I Can Read!** 1 BEGINNING READING

The Berenstain Bears®

God Made the Seasons

Story and Pictures By
Stan & Jan Berenstain with Mike Berenstain

God made the seasons, four in all,

winter, spring, summer, and fall.

In winter we are always told

to put on hats or we'll get cold.

When we go out,

we see our breath.

We see our friends

Fred and Beth.

The snow and ice
are really great!
We can sled!
We can skate!

Mama can do
a figure eight.
Hooray for Mama!
Isn't she great?

Papa, stop!

That ice is thin.

Don't skate there.

You may fall in!

The Bible says, "The winter is past."

Thank you, God. Spring, at last!

Soon signs of spring begin to show.

Bits of green grow through the snow.

Crocuses begin to peep,
waking from their winter sleep.

We see one with a yellow face.
We see robins find a nesting
place.

Robins build a nest
of grass and twigs.

Then Daddy Robin
digs and digs.

He digs for worms
in our yard.
The ground is still
cold and hard.

He finds a worm!

He gets lucky!

You may think that

worms are yucky.

But to robins

they are yummy!

Just right for

a robin's tummy!

God's bright sun climbs high in the sky.

Mom says spring's the reason why.

We get out bikes.

We put back sleds.

Mama weeds the flower beds.

Now the sun is overhead.

Now it's summer, Mama said.

God makes the sun warm all the earth,

and the earth makes plants for all it's worth!

Flowers!

How their colors glow!

You can almost

see them grow!

Mama makes some lemonade.

We will drink it in the shade.

Thank you, God, for all

summer brings—

for lemonade, shade, and

birds that sing!

Here's the lake
where we all swim.
Brother's slow.
I yell at him.

Come on, Brother!

Shake a leg!

Last one in

is a rotten egg!

We swim.

We float.

We wave to someone

in a boat.

We see a fish.

We see a frog.

Look! Is that
an alligator?

No. It's just
a floating log!

"Come out," says Mama.

"You've had enough!"

The clouds float by,

puff by puff.

"Let there be light," the Bible said.

A great big light is overhead.

We feel the sun on our backs.

We eat berries for our snacks.

We feel a breeze.

It's getting cool.

We'll soon be going

back to school.

Summertime is almost gone.

The seasons just keep moving on.

God made the seasons—one, two, three.

What's number four? Now, let us see.

The color of leaves

turns bright and bold.

Yellow!

Red!　　Orange!　　Gold!

Fall is here!

It's all around!

Leaves are falling to the ground!

Winter's coming.
And we all know
what trees stay green
in the snow!

Christmas trees
remind us, friends,
that very soon
the whole year ends.

It's the season of the
Christ Child's birth,
a season of joy for
all the earth.
But, after Christmas,
we will still be here,
all set to start
a brand-new year!

I sought the Lord, and he answered me;
he delivered me from all my fears.
—Psalm 34:4

The Berenstain Bears.

Do Not Fear, God is Near

Story and Pictures By

Stan & Jan Berenstain with Mike Berenstain

When Sister Bear was little
she was afraid of lots of things.

She was afraid of bugs.

She was afraid of birds.

She was afraid of dogs

and thunder and

lightning.

But Sister was most afraid
of spooky shadows.

When Sister got bigger
she understood that trust in God
takes away our fears.

As the Bible says:
"When I am afraid, I put my trust in you.
In God, whose word I praise—
in God I trust and am not afraid."

She was not even afraid
of thunder and lightning!

But Sister was still afraid of
spooky shadows.

"You know, Sister," Mama told her,
"God is always near you,
even when things seem scary."

Brother Bear thought Sister was silly.

He teased her.

"Scaredy bear! Scaredy bear!

Afraid of your own shadow,"

Brother teased.

It was not nice.

But big brothers are not always

nice to little sisters—even Brother Bear.

"That is not nice," said Mama.

"You should be kind to your sister.

As the Good Book says,
'Anyone who withholds kindness
from a friend forsakes the fear
of the Almighty.'"
"That is right," said Papa.
"Besides, Sister is brave about
many other things."

Sister was not afraid of frogs and toads.

She was not afraid of spooky-shaped trees.

And one day when a big spider
came and sat beside her ...

Sister scared the spider away.

But Sister was still scared
of shadows.

She forgot that the Bible says,

"Do not be afraid or discouraged,

for the Lord God, my God, is with you."

"Help!" Sister cried.

"Spooky shadows!"

Sister ran into the tree house

and into Papa's arms.

"We must do something,"
said Mama.
"I have an idea," said Papa.

"Look, Sister," Papa said.
"Shadows can be fun."
He gave her a flashlight
to shine on the wall.

Then Papa made a funny
shadow.

"It looks like a bird,"
said Sister.

Sister looked at Papa's hands.

She looked at the shadow.

Papa wiggled his hands.

The bird flapped its wings.

"It is flapping its wings!" said Sister.

"May I try?"

Papa held the flashlight.

Sister made a bird shadow too.

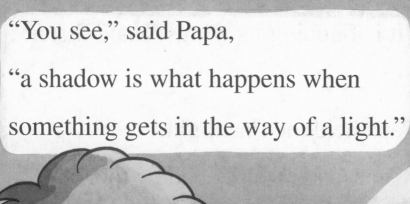

"You see," said Papa,
"a shadow is what happens when
something gets in the way of a light."

Then Papa showed Sister
how to make a shadow rabbit,

a shadow goose,

and a shadow dog.

Later that night, Sister played a trick on Brother.

She made a big shadow bird
and flapped its wings.

"Yipe!" Brother cried.
"A spooky shadow!"

Sister knew she should not tease.
But she wanted to teach
Brother a little lesson.

When they were in bed,

Sister knew she should be kind to Brother.

But she teased him

one more time.

She made a rabbit,
a goose, and a dog.
"Spooky shadows!"
Brother cried.

Papa came in.

"You should not tease your brother," he said.

"But I see you are not afraid of shadows anymore."

"I guess not," Sister said.

But Brother was—a little.

Then he remembered that God

was watching over him.

As the Book of Proverbs says,

"When you lie down, you will not be afraid;

When you lie down, your sleep will be sweet."